藥櫃裡的神秘之旅

Through the Medicine Cabinet

丹・葛林寶（Dan Greenburg）　著／陳亭如　譯
傑克・戴維斯（Jack E. Davis）　繪圖

目次
Contents

聽得下去，才聽得進去

劉經巖

我有一個十歲的女兒和八歲的兒子，過去十幾年，因為工作上的需要與調動，我與家人曾經在不同國家、不同的城市居住過，兩個孩子不但在國外出生，也隨著我經歷了必須橫跨太平洋與大西洋，去找尋下一個家園的日子。這種因為遷就工作調動而經常與其他文化接觸的宿命，固然讓我與孩子得藉以觀察異國文化，增廣視野，這些經年累月的異國生活經驗與見聞，也讓我不得不更加重視在親子教育的努力。因為他們的世界比起一般的孩子更多彩多姿，他們的朋友、同學、玩伴甚至於學校的老師，除了美國人之外，可能是個俄羅斯人，也可能是個印度人；可能來自加拿大，也可能來自加勒比海地區。

我一直希望協助孩子在不同的國度中能怡然自得地面對他們所居處的環境，培養較恢弘的生活視野，同時培育他們兼具東方與西方世界之人文素養與合時宜的價值觀。但最重要的課題仍在於：如何讓他們在成長過程中能瞭解到這個社會裡有真實殘酷的一面，但又不要失去對浪漫理想的追求。

　　因此，儘管工作再忙碌，我儘可能地撥空每晚在孩子入睡前，為他們說上一兩則「床邊故事」，我也花了很多時間跟精神尋找適合他們的床邊故事，從人物傳記、到寓言故事、童話勵志小品等，應有盡有。坊間的童書的確不乏佳作，但許多類似王子與公主從此過著幸福快樂的日子的故事，浪漫得不切實際；或有時講述到頭懸樑、錐刺股的勵志苦讀情節，在今天聽來，除了驚悚，也不太能引發孩子的共鳴，我當然也不會允許他們去效法的。

　　當哈佛人出版社張執行長將「札克檔案」初稿交給我時，我發覺這套書頗有些與眾不同，當我為孩子讀完「札克檔案」第一、二集的初稿，他們的反應是很興奮，而且不停地追問：還有沒有札克故事的續集？

　　兩個孩子的反應讓我產生好奇，仔細分析後發現「札克檔案」是一套在真實生活時空環境下，充滿了想像力與各式新奇有趣事物的故事集，但這套書引人

入勝之處在於，它的驚奇之處與我們生活細節環環相扣，故事鋪陳與發展的過程非常自然，而且故事情節常常出人意表，可謂「情理之中，意料之外」，足以引發孩子濃厚的興趣，因為他們不知道接下來會發生什麼事？因此，這些故事啟發他們的「好奇心」和「想像力」，使他們欲罷不能。

我也觀察到孩子們聽完故事後的反應——他們除了覺得札克的故事很有趣、很好笑之外，還因為他來自於單親家庭而有一點同情他。但我的詮釋是——在札克的世界中（他生長在美國紐約一個單親家庭，是個有點早熟而且EQ頗高的孩子），有大量的獨處時間，也才會發生這麼多稀奇古怪的事情。單親家庭已經是台灣與美國社會甚為普遍的一種家庭型態，我認為作者從單親家庭孩子眼中創造了一個充滿想像的世界，不僅不再讓單親家庭被賦予負面形象，讓這個現象不再象徵一種悲情或是一種禁忌。而或許這也為我們社會開啟了另一種思維方向，不再為單親家庭套上「不快樂的」刻板印象。

從家長的角度來看，我發現札克故事在字裡行間很忠實地介紹了美國社會裡真實的生活層面。像在《我的曾祖父是貓》裡就描述了美國小孩如何到動物收容所辦理領養寵物；又例如到銀行提款時一定要出具當事人證明身分和簽名等金融秩序。而故事中也常不著痕跡地帶出美國的價值觀，例如：莫瑞思曾祖父曾從事各種發明，而發明本身也是一種投資行為；最後他為臘腸狗設計專用的衣服終於為他賺進大筆財富。這些事例讓小孩子看到非常道地的美國精神，那就是一種拓荒冒險精神，勇於創新，鼓勵以創意與投資結合，造就名聲與財富，非常符合資本主義社會的生活基調。

在《藥櫃裡的神秘之旅》當中，提到美國孩子使用牙套的現象（也點出了小孩經常把牙套弄丟的生活插曲）、提到了札克要跟爸爸去參觀洋基隊的春季訓練營等等。這些對美國的孩子來說可是大事，而且是成長過程中不可缺少的大事！這些細微的情節都生動地描繪出小孩發育過程所面臨的一些尷尬以及棒球文化在美國、尤其在美國人父子關係間所具有的一種特殊地位。

　　所以，講述「札克檔案」的過程中，不但與孩子分享充滿想像力的故事，也介紹了美國的生活訊息，更教育了小孩生活中的各種面向。當然，對於曾在美國生活或是擁有大都市生活經驗的人而言，說這些故事是比較駕輕就熟的；但是對於沒有去過美國的人來說，這些故事也可以提供認識美國生活面向的題材。這套書值得推薦的地方也在於——故事中有很多奇怪的構想，雖然會讓你覺得很神奇，但又不至於光怪陸離。

　　這也回應本文最初我所提到的，為孩子挑選適合的讀物是許多父母共同的課題，「札克檔案」最為與眾不同的特色是，它以孩子的眼光看世界，幽默有趣、充滿想像空間；而我的看法是——要讓小孩接受某個教育觀念，首先要讓他們笑、要讓他們開心，他們才會接受這些觀念，而不是嚴肅地說教或說些不切實際的故事。而「札克檔案」就是因為有趣，小孩子聽得下去，裡面所蘊藏的教育內容，他們也才聽得進去。

對那些「想要告訴孩子世界真實面貌，又不希望限制他們發揮想像力而不再嚮往新奇事物，怕孩子變得太世故」的父母親，如果您恰好在書店翻開這本書，何妨駐足瀏覽一番並試著向您的寶貝孩子講述這本書的內容，相信您與孩子都會有意想不到的收穫！

（本文作者目前任職於外交部，曾派駐美國華府、俄羅斯莫斯科等地服務，2004年為外交部選送至哈佛大學甘迺迪政府學院進修，並取得公共行政管理碩士學位。）

Chapter 1

track-1

I'm what you'd call a pretty normal kid. My name is Zack, which is a pretty normal name. I'm ten years old, which is a pretty normal age. I have normal brown hair and eyes. I have slightly crooked teeth, which is normal at my age. And I live in a big apartment building in New York. I always *thought* my building was normal, at least until the thing I'm about to tell you happened.

I've got to admit I've always been interested in weird stuff. Stuff like dead people crawling out of their graves at night. Or guys who stare

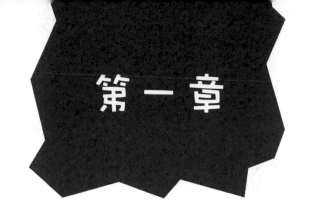

第一章

　　你會覺得我是個很正常的小孩。我叫做札克，也是一個很正常的名字。我今年十歲，是一個很正常的年紀；我有著正常的棕色頭髮與眼睛；我的牙齒長得有點參差不齊，在我的年紀，這也是一件很正常的事。我住在紐約的一棟公寓大樓裡，我以前**自認**為我住的大樓很正常，至少在我即將告訴你的這件事發生之前，我是這麼認為的。

　　老實說，我一直都對搞怪的事情很感興趣，像是半夜裡從墳墓裡爬出來的死人，或

at you and then suddenly their heads explode. I haven't actually seen those things. But who am I to say they couldn't happen?

Anyway, the time I want to tell you about happened at the beginning of spring vacation. My dad arranged to take me down to Florida. We were going to visit the New York Yankees at their spring training camp.

My parents are divorced. Part of the time I live with my dad. He's a writer, and he gets to do lots of cool things. Like go to spring training and then write about it in a magazine. I can't believe he gets paid to do this stuff. Neither can he.

是有人直直地盯著你看，然後他們的頭卻突然爆炸等等。我並沒有親眼見過這種事情，但誰能保證這不會發生呢？

　　不管如何，我想告訴你的這件事情，發生在春假剛開始的時候。我爸爸準備好要帶我去佛羅里達州，訪問正在進行春季訓練營的紐約洋基隊[註]。

　　我的爸媽離婚了，所以有時候，我跟爸爸一起住。他是一個作家，經常可以做很多超酷的事，像是他去春季訓練營採訪，然後發表在雜誌上。我不敢相信他竟然能靠這件事賺錢？他自己也不敢相信。

註：紐約洋基隊（New York Yankees）是美國紐約的職業棒球隊，於1901年成立，距今已有一百多年的歷史。目前知名的台灣投手王建民就是效力於洋基隊，為該隊的主力投手。

Saturday morning was when we were planning to leave. I was so excited, I woke up at about 6:00 A.M. The minute I opened my eyes, I realized something. I had forgotten to put my retainer in my mouth before I went to sleep. Where the heck was it?

A retainer, in case you don't know, is braces that you wear on your teeth at night. I don't exactly love my retainer. It's made of wire and pink plastic. It's really gross-looking, especially when you take it out and put it on the table at lunch.

My dad hates when I lose my retainer.

我們準備在星期六的早上出發，因為我太興奮了，所以大概在早上六點就醒了過來。當我睜開眼睛的那一瞬間，我發現有件事情怪怪的。咋晚睡覺前，我忘記戴上牙套了！那個鬼牙套到底跑哪去了？

牙套（註）就是（以防你不知道的話）——晚上戴在牙齒上的矯正器。我不是真的喜歡我的牙套，它是金屬線與粉紅色塑膠做的，看起來超級噁心，尤其當你吃中飯把它拿下來放在桌上的時候。

老爸最恨我弄丟牙套了。它們得花一千

註：札克戴的牙套屬於活動式，是針對六至十二歲的幼童設計的。因為這個時期的小朋友喪失了乳牙，但是恆牙卻尚未完全萌發，為了維持牙齒空間、顧及美觀與咀嚼功能等等，必須戴這種所謂「混合齒列期的可撤式空間維持器」。

They cost twelve hundred dollars, I think. Or a hundred and twelve. I forget which.

I left one retainer in a pair of jeans, which went in the laundry. It melted to the inside of the pocket. One got chewed up in my Grandma Leah's garbage disposal. Another got flushed down the toilet. Another one I'm almost positive a robber stole while I was out of my room, although I've never been able to prove this.

All in all, I have not lost more than seven of them. Eight, tops.

兩百塊吧，還是一百一十二塊[註1]呢？我忘了到底是哪個價錢了。

我曾經不小心把一個牙套忘在牛仔褲的口袋裡，牛仔褲送洗的時候，牙套在口袋裡融掉[註2]了。有一個是被麗亞奶奶的菜屑處理機[註3]攪碎了；另一個被沖進了馬桶；還有一個，我很確定是有個小偷兒[註4]趁我不在房間的時候偷走它的，雖然我一直沒有辦法證明這件事。

算一算，我弄丟的牙套不超過七個吧，好啦，最多是八個吧！

註1：一塊美金大約等於33塊台幣，所以札克的牙套大約是台幣39,600元，或是3,960元。

註2：這裡的melt不是指札克的牙套真的融化不見了，而是因為烘乾受熱而融得變形了。

註3：美國家庭廚房裡一般在流理台下都會裝有「菜屑處理機」，用來將廚餘攪碎再排入污水管，如此可以減少家庭垃圾的製造量。

註4：英文 robber 原本指的是搶匪，但在此情況指的是小偷。

I was sure my retainer was in the medicine cabinet in the bathroom, instead of in my mouth, where it should have been. I got up and opened the door of the medicine cabinet. Yes! There was my retainer. But then, just as I was about to close the cabinet door, something weird happened. Something very weird. The

我很確定，如果我的牙套沒有在它應該在的地方（就是我的嘴巴裡啦！），那它應該就在浴室的藥櫃^(註)裡。我從床上爬起來，到浴室打開藥櫃。沒錯！我的牙套果然在這兒。但是，當我正要關上藥櫃門的時候，怪事發生了。真的是超怪的！藥櫃的裡

註：在外國，浴室裡洗臉盆上方鑲鏡子的櫃子裡通常都會放一些藥物，因此
　　被稱為藥櫃（medicine cabinet）。

back of the medicine cabinet opened. And there, staring right in my face, was a boy who looked almost exactly like me!

面突然打開了；而且就在裡面，有一個跟我

長得幾乎一模一樣的男孩，正瞪著我看！

Chapter 2

track-2

A boy who looked just like me? How could that be? I was so startled, I knocked over my retainer. It fell into his bathroom. Then we both screamed and slammed our medicine cabinet doors shut.

What the heck was happening here?

Very slowly I opened the medicine cabinet again. Nope. There was nobody on the other side. I pushed against the back of it. It didn't open. Very weird.

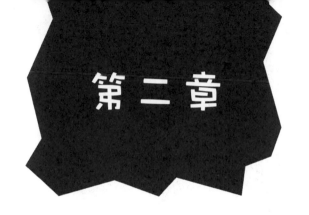

第二章

　　一個跟我長得一模一樣的男孩？怎麼可能啊？我嚇了一大跳，一不小心就撞掉了牙套，掉進了他的浴室裡。我們兩個同時驚聲尖叫，然後大力地把藥櫃門摔上。

　　現在到底是什麼狀況？

　　我又慢慢地打開藥櫃。沒有哇，另一邊一個人也沒有。我推了推藥櫃的裡面，可是打不開，好奇怪喔。

So where was my retainer? I figured I'd better check out the apartment next door. An old lady named Mrs. Taradash lives there.

Mrs. Taradash is kind of cranky. I know she isn't too happy about the basketball hoop I have mounted on my wall. She's complained to my dad lots of times. When I slam-dunk, she says it's like a 5.7 tremor on the Richter scale.

But maybe Mrs. Taradash had a grandson. Maybe her grandson looked almost exactly like me. And maybe her medicine cabinet was hooked up to ours on the other side.

I knew this explanation didn't make much sense. But it was all I could come up with.

　　那我的牙套在哪裡呢？我想我最好去隔壁塔拉太太[註1]的公寓看看。

　　塔拉太太的脾氣有點暴躁。我在牆上架了籃球框讓她很不高興，她向我爸爸抱怨過很多次。每次只要我灌籃，她就感覺像發生了芮氏規模[註2]五點七的大地震似的。

　　說不定塔拉太太有一個孫子，而她的孫子長得跟我幾乎一模一樣。也許她家的藥櫃，和我們家的正好背對背掛在一起，可以相通。

　　我知道這個解釋不太合理，但也只能這樣想了。

註1：「塔拉」原文為Taradash，完整音譯為「塔拉達須」，文中為讓語句較為簡潔，所以簡譯為「塔拉」。

註2：芮氏規模是用來表示地震強度的標度，共分為十級。這個規模最早是由地震學家芮克特（Charles Francis Richter）和古騰堡（Beno Gutenberg）一同制定。

I got dressed. Then I slipped quietly out of our apartment. I knocked on Mrs. Taradash's door. There was no answer. I knocked again. It took a while before somebody opened it. Mrs. Taradash was in a fuzzy robe and fuzzy slippers. Her hair was all messed up. And she was rubbing her eyes. She didn't seem all that thrilled to see me, if you want to know the truth.

"I'm sorry to bother you, Mrs. Taradash," I said. "I was wondering whether I could get my retainer out of your bathroom."

"Your what, precious?" she said.

She calls all kids "precious." But you can tell she doesn't think they are.

　　我穿上衣服，然後靜悄悄地溜出我家。

我敲了敲塔拉太太的門，但是沒有人應門。

於是我又敲了一次，過了好一陣子，終於有

人打開大門了。塔拉太太穿著一件毛茸茸的

袍子與毛茸茸的拖鞋，頭髮亂七八糟的，還

揉著眼睛來應門。我能感覺得出來，她看到

我一點也不高興。

　　「很抱歉打擾您，塔拉太太，」我說。

「我能不能到您的浴室裡，撿回我的牙套

啊？」

　　「小寶貝，你的什麼東西？」她說。

　　她把所有的小孩子叫成「小寶貝」，但

感覺得出來她心裡並不是這麼想的。

"My retainer," I said.

"What in the name of heaven is that, precious?"

"A retainer is braces made out of wire and pink plastic, which sometimes falls down disposals or toilets," I explained. "Mine fell into your apartment when your grandson opened the medicine cabinet door."

Mrs. Taradash looked at me like I was cuckoo.

"I don't have a grandson, precious," she said.

"You don't have a grandson? Then who opened the other side of my medicine cabinet just now?"

「我的牙套。」我說。

「小寶貝，那是什麼玩意兒啊？」

「牙套是一個用金屬線跟粉紅色塑膠做的牙齒矯正器，有時候會掉進菜屑處理機或是馬桶裡，」我向她解釋著，「我的牙套在您孫子打開藥櫃的時候，掉進您的公寓裡了。」

塔拉太太看著我，好像我是一個瘋子。

「小寶貝，我沒有孫子啊！」她說。

「您沒有孫子？那麼剛剛是誰從另一邊打開我的藥櫃呢？」

The bottom half of her face smiled. But the top half was frowning. It looked like both halves were fighting with each other. She tried to close the door on my foot.

"Please don't close the door, Mrs. Taradash," I begged her. "I lost my retainer in your apartment. It's the eighth one that's gotten away from me. Maybe the ninth. If I don't get it back, my dad will kill me. You wouldn't want that on your conscience, would you?"

She opened the door and looked at me.

"What do you want?" she said. It was more hissing than talking. And she seemed to have forgotten the word "precious."

"Just my retainer," I said, "which the boy

她的臉下半部在微笑，但是上半部卻皺著眉頭，看起來好像上下兩邊的臉在打架一樣。她想把門關上。

「塔拉太太，拜託不要關門，」我哀求她。「我的牙套掉在您的公寓裡，這已經是我丟掉的第八個了，說不定是第九個。如果我找不到，我爸會殺了我。您不會忍心看到這種事發生吧，對不對？」

她打開門，然後看著我。

「你到底要什麼？」她說。她不是用說的，而是咬牙切齒擠出聲音來。她好像也忘了說「小寶貝」這個字眼。

「我只要我的牙套而已，」我說，「不

who's not your grandson will tell you fell into your bathroom from my medicine cabinet. Please just let me look for it."

"If I let you look," she said, "will you go away and let me get back to sleep?"

"Yes, ma'am, " I said.

She sighed a deep sigh. Then she waved me into the apartment.

是您孫子的那個男生會告訴您，牙套從我的藥櫃掉進您的浴室裡。拜託拜託讓我找一下就好啦。」

　　「如果我讓你找，」她說，「你就會離開，好讓我回去睡覺嗎？」

　　「會的，女士。」我說。

　　她深深地嘆了一口氣，揮揮手讓我進入她的公寓。

I went in.

Weird. Everywhere you looked, there were stuffed animals. And I don't mean cuddly teddy bears, either. I mean real dead animals that were stuffed by a taxidermist. Squirrels, rabbits, beavers, chipmunks. They were all frozen in weird poses. And they stared at you through their beady glass eyes. They really gave me the creeps.

I hurried into the bathroom and looked around. There was no retainer on the floor or anywhere else. I opened the medicine cabinet. I pushed against the back. It didn't budge. So I

我走了進去。

好奇怪喔！放眼看過去，到處都是填充動物[註]。我指的可不是可愛的泰迪熊喔；我說的是活生生的動物死了以後，由標本師做成的動物標本。有松鼠、兔子、海狸、花栗鼠，牠們都以奇怪的姿勢定住，而且用玻璃眼珠瞪著你看。牠們真的讓我覺得毛骨悚然。

我急忙走進浴室裡，開始四處查看。不管是地板上或者其他地方，都沒有牙套的蹤影。我打開了藥櫃，推了藥櫃的後面，但是

註：stuffed animals原意為「填充動物玩具」。在此指的是動物標本，因為在製作動物標本時，需要先挖掉內臟，再將毛皮浸泡藥水，之後把棉花或其他適合的內容物填塞進動物的體內，就像是填充玩具一般。

closed the medicine cabinet door.

"Satisfied?" she hissed.

I had a sudden feeling that if I didn't leave, her eyes would start glowing red. Then she'd grab me and try to stuff me. There I'd be, standing alongside the other animals in a weird frozen pose, staring at visitors through beady glass eyes.

I apologized and hotfooted it back to my dad's apartment. I didn't have a clue what had happened. I began to think I'd dreamed the whole thing. But if I did, then where was my retainer?

On the way back to my bedroom, I passed

它一動也不動。於是我把藥櫃的門關上了。

「滿意了嗎？」她又從牙縫裡擠出一句話。

我忽然有一種感覺，如果我再不離開的話，她的眼睛會開始發出紅光。然後她會抓住我，把我也變成標本。最後，我也會站在其他動物的旁邊，停在一個奇怪的姿勢，用我的玻璃眼珠瞪著客人。

我向塔拉太太道歉，然後急急忙忙地回到爸爸的公寓。我完全搞不清楚剛剛到底是怎麼一回事，也許整件事情都是我在做夢，但如果是做夢的話，我的牙套跑到哪裡去了呢？

在回房間的途中，我經過浴室，我覺得

my bathroom. Out of the corner of my eye I thought I saw something.

My medicine cabinet door.

It was slowly creeping open.

我的眼角瞄到了什麼。

是我家的藥櫃門。

它居然正慢慢地打開。

Chapter 3

track-3

I raced into my bathroom. I yanked open the door of the medicine cabinet all the way.

There he was! The same boy I'd seen before.

"Hey!" I said.

He didn't slam the door this time. I think he was too stunned. He kept staring. I was staring too. He really did look a whole lot like me. Only his teeth were a lot more crooked.

"Who are you?" I asked.

"Zeke," he said.

"I'm Zack."

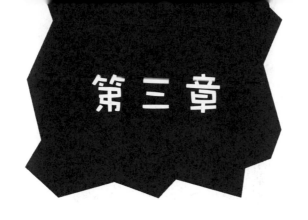

第三章

我衝進浴室，猛力地把藥櫃的門拉開。

就是他！那個我看過的男孩。

「喂！」我說。

他這次沒有把門摔上，我想他也大吃一驚吧！他一直瞪著我，而我也瞪著他。我們長得真的超級像，只是他的牙齒比我的更不整齊。

「你是誰啊？」我問。

「齊克。」他說。

「我是札克。」

"I know."

"You don't live next door," I said. "Do you?"

He shook his head.

"Then where do you live?"

"Someplace else. Someplace nearby, but kind of far away, too. Someplace you might think is weird."

"You live in New Jersey?"

He shook his head.

"Then where?"

"Have you ever heard of Newer York?" he said.

"Is that up near Poughkeepsie?" I asked.

「我知道。」

「你不住在隔壁吧，」我說。「對不對？」

他搖頭。

「那麼，你住在哪裡？」

「某個地方。一個遠在天邊，又近在眼前的地方。一個你可能會覺得很怪的地方。」

「你住在紐澤西州？」

他搖頭。

「那到底是哪裡？」

「你有沒有聽過紐兒約[註1]？」他說。

「是不是靠近波芙鎮[註2]啊？」我問。

註1：原文為Newer York，在此為營造趣味感，故譯為「紐兒約」；亦可譯作「新紐約」，作為故事中對照紐約的平行宇宙。

註2：原文為Poughkeepsie，一般譯為「波啟浦夕」，是位於美國紐約州東部的城市。在此為了使之趣味且簡短，因而譯為「波芙鎮」。

～34～

He sighed and rolled his eyes like I had just said the stupidest thing in the world. I had a sudden thought.

"Hey," I said, "is this something really weird that I'm going to be sorry I got myself involved in?"

"I have time for just one more question," he said. "And then I have to go."

"OK," I said. "Do you have my retainer? I think it fell on your side."

He suddenly tried to slam the door. But I was too fast for him. I stuck my arm into the medicine cabinet. That stopped him from shutting it. He grabbed my hand and tried to pry it off the door. I grabbed his wrist.

　　他嘆了口氣又翻翻白眼，好像我剛剛說了全宇宙最蠢的話。我突然有個想法。

　　「喂，」我說，「這件事是不是真的很怪？怪到再扯下去我一定會後悔的？[註]」

　　「我只有再回答一個問題的時間，」他說，「然後我就要走了。」

　　「好啦，」我說，「我的牙套是不是在你那裡啊？我覺得它好像掉到你那一邊去了。」

　　他突然使力把門關上，但是我的動作比他更快。我把我的手臂伸進藥櫃裡，讓他沒辦法關上門，然後他抓住我的手臂，試著把我的手指從門上扳開，我反過手來抓著他的手腕。

註：這句話其實就是一般常講的「我的好奇心會害了我自己」。

"Let go!" he shouted.

"Not till you give me my retainer!"

He tried to pull away. I held on tight. He backed up. I hung on with both hands. He pulled me through the medicine cabinet. Then we both fell onto the floor in his bathroom.

"Now you've done it!" he shouted. "Now you've really done it!" He looked frightened.

「放開我！」他大喊。

「除非你把牙套還我！」

他試著把手抽開，但我緊緊地抓著他。他往後退，我用雙手緊緊拉住他的手臂。結果，他拖著我穿越了藥櫃，然後我們一起摔在他那邊浴室的地板上。

「看你做的好事！」他大叫著說。「看看你做的好事啦！」他看起來很害怕。

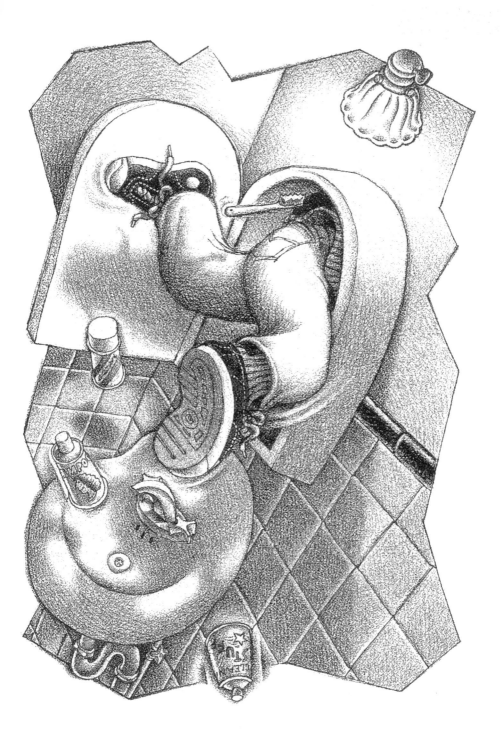

"Done what?" I asked.

"The one thing nobody is ever supposed to do," he said.

"What's that?" I asked.

"Cross over into a parallel universe!"

「做什麼事？」我問。

「不該做的事。」他說。

「那是什麼？」我問。

「你跨進一個平行宇宙了！」

Chapter 4

track-4

"What the heck is a parallel universe?" I asked.

Zeke looked around nervously.

"Shhhh!" he shouted. "Somebody might hear you!"

"You're the one who's shouting," I said. "What the heck is a parallel universe?"

"Well, it's kind of like this," said Zeke. "Our universe is right next to yours. It's so close you wouldn't believe it. It even takes up some of the same space as yours. Only you can't usually see us. Except on Opening Days. Like today."

第四章

「平行宇宙是什麼鬼東西啊？」我問。

齊克緊張兮兮地東張西望。

「噓！」他喊，「有人會聽到你的聲音！」

「是你在大吼大叫耶，」我說，「平行宇宙到底是什麼鬼東西啊？」

「好吧，其實是這樣的，」齊克說，「我們的宇宙就緊貼著你們的宇宙。你很難相信它們會靠得這麼近，甚至我們的宇宙還和你們的共用了某些空間。只是呢，你們通常看不到我們，除了開塞日以外，像今天就是開塞日。」

"Today isn't Opening Day," I said. "The baseball season doesn't start for a couple months yet."

Zeke sighed and shook his head.

"The kind of Opening Day I'm talking about," he said, "has nothing to do with baseball. It's when your universe and mine move right next to each other. It doesn't happen a lot. It'll be years before it happens again."

"Sort of like an eclipse?" I asked.

"Sort of," he said. "When it's Opening Day, we can look through certain openings, like a medicine cabinet. Then we can see your universe. Which, by the way, isn't any better

「今天不是開賽日啦，」我說。「棒球季還要好幾個月才開始呢！」

齊克嘆了一口氣，無力地搖搖頭。

「我說的是開『塞』日，」他說，「跟棒球一點關係都沒有啦！這一天是你們的宇宙跟我們的宇宙剛好移到互相緊接位置的時候。這種情況並不常有，下一次再發生恐怕是很多年以後了。」

「所以，有點像日蝕和月蝕^(註)那樣嗎？」我問。

「有點像啦！」他說。「開塞日那天，我們可以透過某些塞口，譬如說是一個藥櫃，就可以看清楚你們的宇宙。還有，你們

註：「日蝕」是月球運行到太陽與地球的中間時，太陽的光被月球遮擋住部分或全部所形成的現象。而「月蝕」則是地球運行到太陽與月球之間，地球的陰影遮蔽了月球，使月亮上出現黑影的現象。英文的eclipse用來通稱「蝕」這個現象，若要特地指出「日蝕」與「月蝕」，則是用solar eclipse與lunar eclipse。

than ours."

"I didn't say it was better," I said. "Did I say it was better?"

"Maybe not. But I bet that's what you were thinking," he said. "We've got everything you've got. And it's just as good, believe me. Maybe even better."

"OK, OK!" I said. Then I picked myself up off the floor. I got my first good look at the parallel universe in Zeke's bathroom.

Hmmmm.

It looked pretty much the same as mine. Only different. First of all, there was something odd about the sink. There were two faucets. But they were marked Cold and Not So Cold.

的宇宙並沒有比我們的好。」

「我沒有說我們的比較好啊！」我說。
「我有這麼說過嗎？」

「也許沒有。但是我敢打賭你是這麼想
的，」他說。「你們有的東西，我們全都
有。相信我，我們的也一樣好，也許還比你
們的更好呢！」

「好啦，好啦！」我說，然後從地板上
爬起來。我在齊克的浴室裡開始仔細瞧瞧這
個平行宇宙。

嗯──。

他的浴室看起來跟我的滿像的，但是
呢，就是不太一樣。第一，他的洗臉盆怪怪
的，它一樣有兩個水龍頭，只是它們上頭寫
著「冷」和「不太冷」。

Then I looked at the roll of toilet paper by the toilet. It looked like sandpaper. I hoped I wouldn't be in the parallel universe long enough to have to use the bathroom.

I noticed there was a lot of water on the floor. When I glanced at the shower I saw why. Instead of a shower curtain, there were venetian blinds.

"So what's Newer York like?" I asked.

"Outstanding," he said.

"How many channels do you get on TV?" I asked.

He looked at me suspiciously.

"You get more than one channel?" he asked.

然後我看著馬桶旁邊的那卷衛生紙，看起來很像砂紙。我希望我不會在這個平行宇宙裡待到要上廁所。

我注意到地上有很多積水，等我看了淋浴間一眼，我就知道為什麼了。他們不用浴簾，而用一種百葉窗的簾子，一片接一片的。

「紐兒約是個什麼樣的地方呢？」我問。

「超炫的地方。」他說。

「你們的電視有幾個頻道啊？」我問。

他狐疑地看著我。

「你們的頻道不只一個嗎？」他問。

"Never mind," I said.

"Hey," he said. "Everything in the Big Banana is as good as anything you've got in New York."

"Oh, you call Newer York the Big Banana," I said. "Like we call New York the Big Apple."

"Bananas are a lot cooler fruit than apples," he said.

「當我沒說好了。」我說。

「喂，」他說，「大香蕉裡的所有東西就跟紐約的一樣好。」

「喔，你們叫紐兒約大香蕉啊，」我說，「就像我們叫紐約大蘋果(註) 一樣。」

「香蕉可是比蘋果還要酷的水果咧！」他說。

註：大蘋果（Big Apple）是紐約市的俗稱，所以在此作者為紐兒約取名為「大香蕉」用來對應「大蘋果」。

"Look," I said, "I'm sure everything in your universe is every bit as cool as ours, OK? Now can I have my retainer? And then will you please help me cross back over?"

"Zeke, are you packing?" The voice sounded a lot like my dad's.

"Yeah, Dad!" Zeke called back.

"Well, hurry up! The cab is coming at 8:00."

I looked at Zeke strangely.

"You're going somewhere with your dad?" I asked.

"Yeah. We have to catch a plane."

I got a sudden dizzy feeling.

"Your dad isn't by any chance taking you

「聽著，」我說，「我相信你們宇宙裡所有的東西，都跟我們的一樣酷，這樣可以嗎？可以把牙套還給我了嗎？然後可以拜託你幫我爬回去嗎？」

「齊克，你在整理行李了嗎？」那個聲音聽起來很像我老爸。

「是的，老爸！」齊克回應。

「動作快一點！計程車八點就要到了。」

我用怪異的眼神看著齊克。

「你和你爸要出門？」我問。

「對啊！我們得去趕飛機。」

我突然感到一陣暈眩。

「你爸該不會剛好要帶你去紐約洋基隊

to the training camp of the New York Yankees,
is he?" I asked.

"No."

"Well, *that's* a relief," I said.

"He's taking me to the training camp of the
Newer York Yunkees. They're a triple-A minor
league team. But they're just as good as the
Yankees."

"Oh my gosh," I said softly. "Your life is
just the same as mine, except a little different,
isn't it?"

"Well, duh!" he said. "That's what a
parallel universe is, Zack." He sounded like
he was talking to a fourth-grader. I didn't
appreciate that, since I happen to be in the fifth

的訓練營吧？」我問。

「不是。」

「喔，**那真是**讓我鬆了一口氣！」我
說。

「他要帶我去紐兒約勇基隊的訓練營。
他們是小聯盟的三A球隊[註]。不過，他們可
是跟洋基隊一樣強。」

「噢，我的天哪！」我無力地說。「你
的生活跟我的一模一樣，除了有一點點不
同，對不對？」

「噢，笨蛋！」他說，「札克，平行宇
宙就是這麼一回事啊。」他的語氣聽起來好
像在跟小學四年級的學生說話。我可不喜歡
這樣，尤其我已經五年級了。「你想聽實話

註：美國職棒大聯盟底下都會培養數個小聯盟球隊，依照實力高低分為：
　　3A、2A、1A、高階1A、短期1A、新人聯盟等六個等級。這些小聯盟是
　　大聯盟用來培訓旗下球員，或是提供受傷或表現不佳的球員一個復健及
　　比賽機會的訓練系統。

grade. "You want to know the truth? I'm a little tired of living in the one that's the copy and not the one that's the original."

"You are? But you just said—"

"Never mind what I said. I may live in a parallel universe. But I'm not stupid. Don't you think I'd rather be going to see the Yankees train than the Yunkees?"

"I can't hear you, Zeke!" called his dad. "Are you talking to me?"

"No, to myself!" he shouted. Then to me he said, "Hey, I've got an idea. Why don't we switch places? I'll go to the Yankees' training camp with your dad. You can go to the Yunkees' with mine."

嗎？我住在這個盜版的平行宇宙裡已經厭煩了。」

「你覺得煩嗎？你剛剛不是說——」

「不要管我剛剛說什麼。我是住在一個平行宇宙裡沒錯，但我可不是笨蛋。你以為我不會比較想看洋基隊受訓，而會想看勇基隊嗎？」

「齊克，我聽不清楚你在說什麼！」他爸叫道。「你在跟我說話嗎？」

「不是啦，我在自言自語！」他喊道。然後他轉向我說：「喂！我有一個主意。不然我們來交換身份好了，我跟你爸去洋基隊的訓練營，你可以跟我爸去勇基隊的。」

"No way," I said.

"Never mind," he said. "I didn't want to do it anyway."

"Have you packed your retainer yet?" called Zeke's dad.

"Don't worry about it!" Zeke answered nervously.

"Oh my God," I said. "Don't tell me you can't find your retainer either!"

"So what?" he said.

This was freaking me out.

"Zeke," called his dad. He sounded like he was right outside the door. "Are you in there?"

Zeke looked scared.

「才不要！」我說。

「算了，」他說。「反正我也不想這麼做。」

「你的牙套帶了沒？」齊克的爸爸叫道。

「你不用擔心啦！」齊克緊張地回答。

「我的老天啊！」我說。「別跟我說，你也找不到你的牙套啊！」

「那又怎樣？」他說。

這真是把我嚇到了。

「齊克，」他爸爸叫道，聽起來他好像就在門外了。「你在裡面嗎？」

齊克看起來很慌張。

"We can't let him see you here," he whispered. "You've got to hide!"

"Where?"

"Here."

He led me to the bathtub. He pulled back the blinds and pushed me inside. Then I heard him open and close the medicine cabinet door. And then nothing. What was he up to?

「不能讓他看到你在這裡，」他小聲地說。「你必須躲起來！」

「躲在哪裡？」

「躲這裡！」

他把我帶到浴缸旁邊，把百葉簾拉開後就把我往裡面推。然後我聽到他把藥櫃打開又關起來的聲音。之後就什麼聲音都聽不到了。他到底在幹嘛？

I looked at my watch. I had only a half hour before our cab came. What was I doing hiding in a bathtub in a parallel universe? And how was I ever going to get back to mine?

I peeked through the blind. Zeke was nowhere in sight. And then I knew.

That little rat had sneaked back through the medicine cabinet door into my universe!

　　我看了看我的手錶，離計程車來的時間只剩下半個小時。我怎麼還躲在平行宇宙的浴缸裡呢？我到底要怎麼樣才能回到我自己的宇宙呢？

　　我透過簾子偷偷往外看，到處都看不到齊克。然後，我知道發生什麼事了！

　　那個可惡的小賊趁機爬進藥櫃，跑到我的宇宙去了！

Chapter 5

I was in a panic.

At this very minute, Zeke was pretending to be me. He was getting ready to leave with my dad for the Yankee training camp in Florida!

I heard a knock at the bathroom door.

"Zeke, did you hear me? Are you ready?" said his father's voice.

I held my breath.

The door opened. Zeke's father came into the bathroom. Just then I sneezed.

"Achooooo!"

第五章

我陷入一陣恐慌。

就在此時此刻，齊克假裝是我。他正準備跟我爸爸出發去佛羅里達州的洋基隊訓練營！

浴室門傳來敲門聲。

他爸爸的聲音傳了過來：「齊克，你有沒有聽到我說的話？你準備好了沒有？」

我憋住氣。

門打開了，齊克的爸爸走進浴室，就在這個時候，我打了個噴嚏。

「哈啾——！」

"Zeke? Are you in the shower?"

"No, sir," I said.

The blinds were pulled up. There stood a dad who looked almost exactly like mine.

At first I was scared he might be mad. But then he began to laugh.

"What are you doing in the shower with your clothes on?" he asked.

"Resting," I said.

"There's no time for resting, Zeke. Our cab is coming in about half an hour. Have you got your retainer? Are you all packed?"

"Pretty much," I said.

He looked at me oddly and frowned.

「齊克，你在洗澡嗎？」

「沒有，先生。」我說。

簾子被拉了起來，一個長得幾乎跟我爸一模一樣的人站在那邊。

一開始我很怕他會生氣，可是他卻開始笑了起來。

「你穿著衣服在淋浴間裡幹嘛？」他問道。

「我正在休息。」我說。

「齊克，你沒時間休息了。再過半小時左右，我們的計程車就會到。你的牙套收好了沒有？行李都打包好了嗎？」

「差不多了。」我說。

他神情詭異地看著我，皺著眉頭。

"You look a little different, son. Did you comb your hair a new way this morning?"

"Yes, sir. I did. That's exactly what I did."

"Uh huh. OK. Well, I still have a few things to do. Zeke, could you run to the dry cleaners quickly and pick up all our cleaning?"

The cleaners! The only place I wanted to go was back through the medicine cabinet. But what could I say?

"Uh, s-sure," I stammered. "What cleaners would that be again?"

"You know. The one across the street and down the block."

"Uh huh. And what block would that be again?"

「兒子，你看起來有點兒不一樣。你今天早上是不是梳了一個新髮型？」

「是沒錯，先生。是那樣沒錯。」

「嗯哼，好吧。我還有幾件事情要處理。齊克，你可以跑去洗衣店，然後把我們的衣服都拿回來嗎？」

洗衣店！我唯一想去的地方，就是穿過藥櫃回家去。但我又能說什麼呢？

「嗯，好——好啊，」我結結巴巴地說。「能不能再說一次，是哪一家洗衣店啊？」

「你知道的啊，過了馬路再沿著街一直走就會到的那一家。」

「嗯哼，是哪一條街啊？」

He looked at me and raised an eyebrow.

"C'mon," he said. "You've gone there lots of times. Just get going. We have to leave soon."

"OK," I said.

He handed me a receipt and a twenty-dollar bill. Then he walked out of the bathroom.

The twenty-dollar bill looked strange. It was enormous. And when I examined it closely, I saw that along the top it said "The Untied States of America." The picture on all the twenty-dollar bills I've seen is of Andrew Jackson. This one was of somebody with bushy

他看著我，然後挑了挑眉毛。

「拜託！」他說。「你已經去過那裡很多次了，動作快點！我們要快點出發了！」

「好吧。」我說。

他拿了一張單據給我，還有一張二十元的美鈔，然後他走出了浴室。

那張二十元的鈔票看起來很奇怪，它好大張喔！當我仔細檢查它的時候，我發現沿著紙鈔的上端寫著「美利堅分散國[註1]」。我所看過的二十元美金鈔票上頭的人像都是安德魯‧傑克遜[註2]。但是這一張上面的

註1：原文為The Untied States of America，是取自The United States of America（美利堅合眾國），untied是「解除的；鬆開的」之意，恰好與united表示「團結的」之意相反，兩個字只有 t 與 i 的順序不同。

註2：安德魯‧傑克遜（Andrew Jackson）是美國的軍事英雄和第七任總統。

hair, a beard, and nose-glasses. His name was

Slappy Kupperman.

I left the apartment and went down in the

elevator. Then I got outside. I wanted to get to

the cleaners and back as fast as I could.

At the corner I waited for traffic to stop.

It was taking forever. Then I looked up at the

traffic signal and I saw why. Instead of a red

and a green light, there were four lights.

The lights said, "STOP," "NOT YET,"

"HOLD ON," and "OK, GO ALREADY."

Newer York sure was a weird place.

A big billboard to my right said, "WE

人，是一個有著濃密頭髮、大鬍子，還戴著
夾鼻子眼鏡的傢伙。他的名字是史萊痞・酷
佩門。

我走出公寓門，搭電梯下樓，然後走到
外面去。我想趕快去洗衣店，然後再趕回
來。

我在街角等待車輛停下來，但好像永遠
等不到綠燈。我抬頭看看紅綠燈，才知道為
什麼會這麼久了。這個紅綠燈有四盞燈，而
不是一般的一紅一綠。

四個燈號上頭寫著：「停」、「還不
行」、「等一下」，以及「好了，快走
吧！」。

紐兒約果然是一個超怪的地方啊！

我的右手邊有一個大型的看板，它寫

LOVE NEWER YORK! JUST AS GOOD AS NEW YORK. MAYBE BETTER!" Well, I didn't think so. I wanted to get back to my own universe.

I did manage to find the cleaners. I got Zeke's dad's clothes. Then I beat it out of there. I went back down the block. But I must have gotten messed up somehow. Because when I

著：「我們愛紐兒約！就和紐約一樣棒，也許，更棒喔！」嗯，我可不這麼認為。我真想趕快回到我的宇宙去。

我還是找到了洗衣店，拿了齊克爸爸的衣服，然後就趕緊離開了。我沿著那條街往回走，但是一定在哪裡走錯了。因為當我走

got to the corner, the big billboard should have been to my left. But it wasn't there at all.

I took a quick look around. Nothing looked familiar. Then I saw a big apartment building across the street. It had a fancy canopy. It looked a whole lot like one in my own neighborhood in my own universe. The Beekman Arms Plaza Apartments. I thought maybe the doorman could help me find my way back to Zeke's. The problem was, I didn't even know Zeke's stupid address. All I knew was that it would probably be like mine. Only a little different.

I ran to the building. But there wasn't any doorman. In fact, there wasn't even any

到街角，發現那個本來應該在我左手邊的大型看板，居然不見了。

我迅速地看看四周，所有的東西看起來都很陌生。然後我看見馬路對面有一棟大型的公寓建築，它有一個很華麗的遮雨篷。那棟大樓看起來，很像我的宇宙裡的某一棟大樓，而且就在我家附近。它叫畢克曼・阿姆斯廣場公寓大樓。我想或許那裡的管理員可以幫我找到回齊克家的路；但問題是，我連齊克家的鬼地址都不知道。我只知道可能跟我家的住址很像，就只有一點點不一樣吧！

我跑到那棟大樓，但是並沒有管理員。事實上，那裡根本就沒有什麼大樓！我眼前

building! What I thought was a building was only a fake front, like a movie set. The bushes in front of it were made of green plastic. There was a tag on them. It said, "Realistic bushes. Last longer. Need less care. Better than real."

I gulped. I felt like I was in a dream. One of those really awful ones where, no matter how hard you try to get someplace, you can't, and then you puke.

In the middle of the street I saw an open manhole. There were police barricades around it. Signs said, "DANGER ON OPENING DAYS! FALLING IN WOULD BE STUPID! ALSO PAINFUL! DID WE MENTION ILLEGAL?"

札克檔案
藥櫃裡的神秘之旅

的大樓，其實只是一面牆，就像電影的佈景一樣！這道牆的前面有一排綠色塑膠做的灌木叢。上面掛著一個牌子，寫著：「逼真的灌木叢，活得更久，更不需要照顧，比真的更好。」

我倒吸了一口氣。我感覺好像在一個夢境裡，而且是那種超級糟糕的惡夢，不管你多努力想要去哪裡，你都去不成，然後你忍不住就吐了。

在路的正中間，我看見一個打開著的下水道出入孔^(註)，旁邊有警示路障圍繞著。還有牌子寫著：「**開塞日危險！掉進去會很蠢！而且很痛！更別忘了這是不合法的！**」

註：manhole不只是地面上才會有，只要藏有地下管線的工程結構，例如橋樑或是隧道等等，都會設置「地下管線人員出入孔」讓維修等相關工作人員進出，又簡稱為「人孔」。

～78～

Hey! This could be another way to get back to my universe! If I couldn't find my way back to Zeke's and go through the medicine cabinet, maybe I could climb through here. Going through the sewers would be pretty gross, of course. But I didn't care. At least I'd come out on the right side.

I waited for the traffic light to change. Again it took forever. Then I raced up to the manhole. Now was the time to make my move. But just as I stooped down, I felt a heavy hand on my shoulder.

I looked up. A big policeman was standing over me. He seemed kind of scary. But then I looked at the gun in his holster. It was a Super Soaker.

嘿！這也許是另一個可以回去我的宇宙的方法！如果我找不到回齊克家的路，沒辦法從藥櫃回去，或許我可以從這裡爬回去。當然，穿越下水道會滿噁心的，不過我不在乎了！至少我會回到我的宇宙。

我等著紅燈變綠，這一次又等了非常久。然後我衝向那個出入孔，現在是我採取行動的時候了！但是正當我彎下腰的時候，我感覺有一隻大手放在我的肩膀上。

我抬起頭來，有一個體型巨大的警察站在我的身旁。他看起來有點可怕。但是我看到他手槍皮套裡的槍，竟然是一支大水槍耶！

"You wouldn't want to get too close and fall into New York," he said. "Now would you, sonny?"

"Oh boy, sir. I sure wouldn't want to do that," I said.

We both laughed pretty hard at the idea I'd want to do anything as stupid as fall into New York.

"Well then, step away from there," he said.

I did. He stayed right next to the manhole. I don't think he trusted me. But with his Super Soaker he didn't seem so scary anymore. I decided to ask his help.

"Um, Officer," I said, "I'm kind of lost. I was on my way home. But I must have taken a wrong turn or something."

「你別靠得太近，小心掉進紐約裡
去，」他說。「你說對不對啊，小朋友？」

「喔不，先生，我當然不會想這麼做
的。」我說。

我們兩個人一起狂笑，因為我居然會笨
到想要掉進紐約裡去！

「既然這樣，快點離開那裡！」他說。

我照著他的話走開了。他還留在出入孔
旁邊，我想他不相信我。但是他帶著大水
槍，看起來實在不怎麼可怕。所以，我決定
求他幫個忙。

「嗯，警察先生，」我說，「我想我迷
路了。我正要回家，但是我一定是轉錯了
彎，還是走錯路什麼的。」

"What's your address, son?" he asked.

"My address?"

"Yes."

"Uh, well, I'm not exactly sure," I said. "I mean it seems to have temporarily slipped my mind."

"Your address has slipped your mind?"

"Temporarily."

He looked at me strangely. But he listened while I described Zeke's building.

"Oh, I know the one you mean," he said. "I'll take you there."

He took me by the hand. Then he led me down the block and around the corner.

There it was, Zeke's building! I thanked

「小朋友，你家的地址是什麼？」他問。

「我家的地址？」

「是啊。」

「嗯，我不太確定耶，」我說。「我是說，我好像暫時忘記了。」

「你忘了你家的地址？」

「暫時忘了。」

他莫名其妙地看著我，但還是聽著我描述齊克住的大樓。

「喔，我知道你說的是哪裡，」他說。「我帶你去。」

他牽起我的手，然後帶著我沿著街走到下一個路口再轉一個彎。

齊克家的大樓就在那裡！我滿懷感激地

him all over the place, and then I took off. He was probably glad to get rid of me.

Right in front of Zeke's building was a newsstand. It was just like the one in front of my own building. On the front page of all the newspapers were big headlines:

"DANGER! OPENING DAY ARRIVES! CITIZENS WARNED NOT TO TAKE CHANCES!"

向他道謝，然後我就跑掉了。他大概也很高興可以甩掉我吧。

齊克家的大樓前面有一個書報攤，看起來就和我家門口的那個攤子長得一樣。所有的報紙頭條都寫著：

「危險！開塞日來臨了！警告市民切勿冒險！」

Danger? What danger? I picked up a paper and started to read.

"Today, in the early hours of the morning, citizens of Newer York will once again be able to peek through any of several openings and actually observe life in our sister universe. 'Do not attempt to cross over into the alternate universe!' warns Professor Roland Fenster at the Newer York Institute of Parallel Universes. 'The openings should appear somewhere in the vicinity of 6:00 A.M. They will then shut down tight again approximately two hours later. Once shut, they will not reopen for as many as thirty years. Thirty years would be one heck of a long time to spend in a universe that's rumored to be better than ours, but isn't.' "

危險？什麼危險呢？我起拿一份報紙來看。

「今天清晨起，紐兒約的市民可以再一次透過幾個塞口，觀察平行宇宙的生活。紐兒約平行宇宙研究院的羅蘭‧芬史特教授忠告市民：『不要企圖越入另一個宇宙。大約在清晨六點時，某些地方會有塞口開啟，大約兩個小時之後關閉。一旦塞口關閉，將有三十年的時間不會再開啟。在那個宇宙生活三十年會是一段可怕的漫長時光，謠傳說紐約比我們好，但實際上並不是這麼一回事！』」

I looked at my watch. Yikes! It was 7:45
A.M. I had just fifteen minutes before the cab
came and Zeke left for Florida with my dad.
And before the doors to my universe slammed
shut for thirty years!

I raced into Zeke's building.

　　我看了一下我的手錶。天哪！已經是上午七點四十五分了，只剩十五分鐘，計程車就會來接齊克和我爸爸到佛羅里達州去了！而且能夠返回我的宇宙的塞口也將關上三十年！

　　我飛快地衝回齊克的大樓。

Chapter 6

track-6

I arrived back in Zeke's apartment out of breath. I dropped Zeke's dad's cleaning in the hallway. I raced into the bathroom.

I pushed hard against the back of the medicine cabinet. But I couldn't make the darned thing budge. Zeke obviously knew more about traveling between universes than I did!

And then I heard somebody behind me. I whirled around to find Zeke's dad looking at me strangely.

"Zeke," he said, "what are you doing?"

Should I tell him the truth? Could I trust

第六章

我氣喘吁吁地回到齊克的公寓。我把齊克爸爸的衣服丟在走廊上，然後衝進浴室。

我用力地推著藥櫃的裡面，但是我完全沒辦法移動這該死的東西。很明顯地，齊克比我還更了解如何在兩個宇宙間穿梭旅行！

然後我聽到有人在我背後，我轉身發現齊克的爸爸正神情詭異地看著我。

「齊克，」他說，「你在做什麼？」

我該告訴他真相嗎？我可以相信他嗎？

him? Or was he the enemy? I didn't know. But time was running out. And I didn't see that I had much choice.

"Listen, sir," I said, "this is going to sound sort of incredible. But it's the truth, so help me."

"All right, Zeke," he said. "But make it fast. We have less than fifteen minutes before the cab comes."

"OK," I said. "First of all, I'm not your son, Zeke. I'm somebody else who looks just like him. And my name is Zack. I live in the parallel universe. My dad and I were getting ready to go to the Yankees' training camp. Just like you and Zeke were getting ready to go to the Yunkees'

他是不是敵人呢？我不知道。但時間正一分

一秒地過去，我好像沒有什麼選擇啊！

「先生，請聽我說，」我說，「這件事

聽起來有點兒不可思議，但這是真的！所以

請幫幫我吧！」

「好吧，齊克，」他說，「不過，你要

說快一點，計程車不到十五分鐘就到了。」

「好啦，」我說，「第一點，我不是你

兒子齊克，我只是一個長得像他的人。還

有，我的名字叫做札克，我住在平行宇宙

裡。我爸和我正準備出發去洋基隊的訓練

營，就像你跟齊克準備去勇基隊的訓練營一

training camp. Only I dropped my retainer through the medicine cabinet. I lost it, the same as Zeke lost his."

Zeke's dad's mouth dropped open. He smacked his forehead with his hand.

"I can't be-lieve it!" he said.

"It's true, though, sir," I said. "I swear."

"Zeke has lost his retainer?" he said in a dazed voice. "That's the tenth one so far this year."

Wow! Zeke was even worse than me!

"Do you know how much those things cost?" he asked.

"Either twelve hundred dollars or a hundred and twelve dollars," I said quickly.

樣。只是我的牙套穿過藥櫃掉進來了，我搞丟了牙套，就像齊克也弄丟他的一樣。」

齊克的爸爸嘴巴張得開開的，他用自己的手「啪！」地一聲拍打著他的額頭。

「我真是不敢相——信啊！」他說。

「但是，這是真的，先生，」我說，「我發誓。」

「齊克弄丟了他的牙套？」他用像是快要暈倒的口氣說道。「那已經是今年的第十個了！」

哇，齊克比我還糟糕嘛！

「你知道那些東西要花多少錢嗎？」他問道。

「如果不是一千兩百塊，就是一百一十二塊，」我很快地說著，「但你有

"But didn't you hear the other stuff I told you?"

"Yes, yes, yes. Of course I did," he said. "Your name is Zack. You live in the parallel universe on the other side of the medicine cabinet, blah, blah, blah."

"You don't believe me, do you?" I said.

"Why shouldn't I believe you?" he said. "Everybody in Newer York knows about

沒有聽到我講的另一件事呢？」

「有，有，有，我當然有！」他說。「你的名字叫札克，你住在藥櫃另一邊的平行宇宙啦！巴啦，巴啦……諸如此類的事情吧。」

「你不相信我，對不對？」我問。

「我為什麼不相信你？」他說，「紐兒約所有的人都知道你們的宇宙，這又不是什

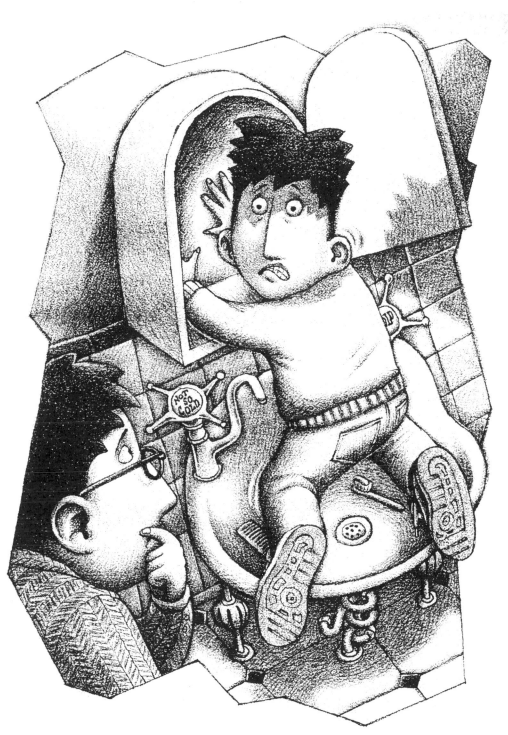

your universe. It's not like it's a big secret or anything. And it isn't any better than ours either, by the way."

Boy, this was a touchy subject with these guys!

"I never said it was better," I said. "Look, sir, you seem to know a lot about parallel universes. So maybe you know how to slip back through the medicine cabinet to mine. Like Zeke did just now."

"Zeke?" he said. "He crossed over?"

I nodded. I really had Zeke's dad's attention now.

"But it's almost 7:50!" Zeke's dad smacked his forehead again. "At 8:00 Opening Day will

麼了不起的秘密。再說，你們的宇宙也沒有
比我們的好。」

　　天哪！對這些人來說，這可真是個敏感
的話題呢！

　　「我從沒說過我們的比較好，」我說，
「聽著！先生，你好像知道很多有關平行宇
宙的事情。所以，你可能知道我該怎麼穿過
藥櫃回去我的宇宙，就像齊克剛剛做的一
樣。」

　　「齊克？」他說，「他穿過去了？」

　　我點點頭，這下子我真的引起齊克老爸
的注意了。

　　「但是現在已經快要七點五十分了！」
齊克的爸爸又拍一下他的額頭，「開塞日會

shut down completely!"

"My point exactly, sir," I said. "I'd be miserable if that happened. Not that I wouldn't love living here, I mean. Because I think it's at least as good as my universe. And maybe even better. But the thing is, I'd really miss my mom and dad."

"OK, OK," said Zeke's dad. "This is what you have to do. Put your hand on the back wall of the medicine cabinet."

I did.

"Close your eyes. Take a deep breath. Now visualize the back wall opening. Let me know if you feel anything."

I did everything he said. It started to work.

在八點鐘完全結束啊！」

「這就是我的重點啊，先生，」我說。
「如果發生了那樣的事情，我會非常痛苦
的。我不是說我不喜歡住在這裡，因為我知
道這裡至少跟我的宇宙一樣好，甚至更好！
但是，我會很想念我的媽媽和爸爸。」

「好啦！好啦！」齊克的爸爸說道。
「你必須這樣做——把你的手放在藥櫃裡邊
的牆上。」

我照做了。

「閉上你的雙眼，深呼吸。現在，想像
牆上出現了一個開塞口，讓我知道你有沒有
感覺到什麼。」

我照著他的指示做。咦，開始有效了！

The wall was starting to feel kind of springy.
I opened my eyes in time to see it sort of melt
away.

那面牆開始有點彈性的感覺，我張開雙眼

時，剛好看到它融成一道開口。

Chapter 7

"**H**i, Zack," said a familiar face.

"Zeke!" said Zeke's dad. "Oh, thank heavens!"

"Zeke," I said. "Were you coming back?"

He looked embarrassed.

"I got homesick, " he said. "I mean, your dad is awfully nice, Zack. He really is. But he's not my dad. And this isn't my universe. I figured you must feel the same way. Even though Newer York is just as cool as New York."

My dad appeared on the other side of the medicine cabinet.

第七章

「嗨，札克！」一個熟悉的面孔說道。

「齊克！」齊克的爸爸說，「喔，謝天謝地！」

「齊克！」我說，「你要回來了嗎？」

他看起來有點尷尬。

「我想回家了！」他說，「我是說，札克，你爸人超好的，他真的很好。但是他不是我爸爸。而且這不是我的宇宙。我想你一定也這麼覺得吧！雖然，紐兒約跟紐約一樣酷。」

我爸爸出現在藥櫃的另一邊。

"Dad!" I said.

"Hi, Zack," said my dad. Then he turned to Zeke's dad. "Hi, Don," he said. "Long time, no see."

"Hi, Dan," said Zeke's dad to my dad.

They shook hands through the medicine cabinet.

"You two *know* each other?" I asked, amazed.

「老爸！」我說。

「嗨，札克！」我爸爸說。然後他轉向齊克的爸爸。「阿當，你好啊！」他說，「好久不見了！」

「嗨！阿丹。」齊克的爸爸對我爸爸說。

他們透過藥櫃握了握手。

「你們兩個認識啊？」我驚訝地問。

"Yeah, we met when we were your age," said Zeke's dad. "But it wasn't through a medicine cabinet. It was through a dryer in the laundromat."

"Yeah," said my dad. "I always wondered what happened to odd socks that got lost in the laundry. Who'd have guessed they go to the parallel universe?"

"That was quite an Opening Day," said Zeke's dad. "Not much laundry got dried. But we sure had fun. Your dad thought I lived in the dryer."

Both my dad and Zeke's dad started laughing their heads off.

"Uh, excuse me for interrupting," I said.

「對啊！我們在你們這個年紀的時候碰過面，」齊克的爸爸說，「但不是透過藥櫃，而是經過自助洗衣店裡的乾衣機。」

「對啊！」我爸爸說，「我常常納悶，那些在洗衣店裡洗到剩一隻的襪子到底去哪裡了？誰會猜得到它們跑到平行宇宙裡去了？」

「那是一個很特別的開塞日，」齊克的爸爸說道，「沒烘乾幾件衣服，但我們卻玩得很愉快，你爸爸還以為我住在乾衣機裡頭呢！」

老爸跟齊克的爸爸開始捧腹大笑。

「呃，很抱歉打斷你們哪！」我說。

"This is all very interesting. But it's now 7:55."

"Oh, right, right!" said Zeke's dad. He looked through the cabinet at Zeke. "Do you still want to go to the Yunkees' training camp, son?"

"I sure do!" said Zeke.

"Then let me pull you through," said Zeke's dad.

So Zeke crawled back into his own universe. I crawled back into mine.

"I'm sorry, Zack," said Zeke. "I was a real jerk."

"You were," I said. "But I forgive you."

Cab horns were now honking on both sides of the cabinet.

「這些事情都很有趣，但是現在已經是七點五十五分了。」

「喔，對喔，對喔！」齊克的爸爸說道。他透過藥櫃看著齊克，「兒子，你還想去勇基隊的訓練營嗎？」

「我當然想啊！」齊克說。

「那我把你拉過來囉！」齊克的爸爸說。

齊克爬回去他的宇宙，我也爬回我的。

「札克，對不起，」齊克說，「我可真是一個笨蛋！」

「你是啊，」我說，「不過我原諒你。」

計程車的喇叭聲在藥櫃的兩邊同時響起。

"Well, so long, guys," I said.

"See you again sometime," said Zeke.

"Maybe at the next Opening Day," I said.

"OK," said Zeke.

He fished something out of his pocket. He handed it to me through the cabinet. It was my retainer!

"You swiped my retainer?" I said.

He nodded sheepishly.

"But I couldn't keep it," he said.

"Because you knew it was wrong."

"Yeah," he said. "Also, it didn't fit."

Then all of a sudden, the grandfather clock in our hallway started chiming.

It was 8:00.

「再見囉！朋友們。」我說。

「有機會再見囉！」齊克說。

「也許在下一個開塞日吧！」我說。

「好！」齊克說。

他從口袋裡掏出一樣東西，穿過藥櫃拿給我。那是我的牙套！

「你摸走了我的牙套？」我說。

他慚愧地點點頭。

「可是我不能將它占為己有。」他說。

「因為你知道這樣做是不對的。」

「嗯，」他說，「而且這個牙套和我的嘴巴不合。」

突然間，走廊上的老爺鐘開始噹噹作響。

八點鐘了。

We waved good-bye to each other.
Then, instead of facing Zeke and his dad, I
was looking at shelves with toothpaste and
deodorant. I pushed hard against the back wall
of the medicine cabinet. I visualized like crazy.
But nothing happened.

So that's how I discovered the parallel
universe. And every time I open my medicine
cabinet, I think of Zeke and his dad. I kind of
miss them. It's funny to think that they're so
close, and yet so far away.

The next time I see Zeke, I could have a
son of my own. Weird! I wonder what he'll be
like. Hey, wouldn't it be cool if he's just like

　　我們互相揮手道別。原本我面前是齊克和他的爸爸，但是突然之間，眼前只有擺放著牙膏與除臭劑的架子。我用力推著藥櫃裡面的牆，瘋狂地想像著，可是什麼事都沒發生。

　　這就是我發現平行宇宙的經過。後來，我每次打開藥櫃的時候，我都會想起齊克和他的爸爸。我有點兒想念他們，只要一想到他們是這麼地靠近卻又遙遠，我就會覺得很有趣。

　　下一次再看到齊克，我可能也有自己的兒子了。真的超怪的！我在想，他會是什麼樣子呢？如果他長得跟我一模一樣，不就酷

me? In every way except one: I hope he doesn't

ever need to wear a retainer!

斃了嗎？只有一件事例外：我希望他永遠都
不必戴牙套！

札克檔案02

藥櫃裡的神秘之旅

原著作者	丹·葛林寶（Dan Greenburg）
譯　　者	陳亭如（Ting Chen）
出版公司	哈佛人出版有限公司（H. I. Publishers, Inc.）
執 行 長	張錦娥（Gina Chang）
文　　編	趙曉南（Nadia Chao）・閻若婷（Michelle Wen） 郭啓宏（Arthur Kuo）・洪采薇（Therisa Hung）
地　　址	110 台北市信義區基隆路一段380號6樓
電　　話	02-2725-1823
傳　　真	02-2725-5962
Blog	http://tw.myblog.yahoo.com/harvard_inspired/
E-mail	harvard_inspired@yahoo.com.tw
會計稅務顧問	呂旭明會計師
總 代 理	農學股份有限公司
出版日期	西元2007年12月 初版二刷
定　　價	新台幣199元

國家圖書館出版品預行編目資料

藥櫃裡的神秘之旅／丹·葛林寶（Dan
Greenburg）著；傑克·戴維斯（Jack　E.
Davis）繪；陳亭如譯. --初版. -- 台北
市：哈佛人，2007〔民96〕
面；　公分. --（札克檔案；2）
中英對照
譯自：Through the Medicine Cabinet
ISBN 978-986-7045-15-7（平裝附光碟）

874.59　　　　　　　　　95002012